RIDE A COCK-HORSE
TO BANBURY CROSS

 Grolier Educational Corporation

RIDE a Cock-Horse
to Banbury Cross,

To see a fine Lady

Get on a white Horse,

With rings on her fingers,

and bells on her toes,

She shall have music wherever she goes.

A Farmer went trotting

UPON HIS GREY MARE

A FARMER went trotting upon his grey Mare;

Bumpety, bumpety, bump!

With his Daughter behind him, so rosy and fair;

Lumpety, lumpety, lump!

A Raven cried ''Croak!'' and they all tumbled down;

Bumpety, bumpety, bump!

The Mare broke her knees, and the Farmer his crown;

Lumpety, lumpety, lump!

The mischievous Raven flew laughing away;

Bumpety, bumpety, bump!

And vowed he would surprise them the very next day;

Lumpety, lumpety, lump!